KU-757-106

MOG IN THE FOG

for Tom

MOG in the FOG

by Helen Nicoll
and Jan Pieńkowski

PUFFIN BOOKS

Goodbye Owl
Why won't you come?

Are we nearly there?
Mog wanted to climb th

highest mountain in the world

A Sherpa saw them land

Hello
I'm Tsing
This is Yak
I'm Meg
This is Mog
Yak
Meeow

Will you take us to the top?
O.K. I lead caravan

Oh dear oh dear
Very old bridge
CREAK
They crossed
many torrents

Up and up and up they climbed

It
started
to
snow

Tsing took them to a cave

Good tea! Good butter in it
Yuk!
?

The sun
came out.
It was
dazzling

Mog found some footprints

Mog! Mog!
Where are
you?

A huge cloud came down

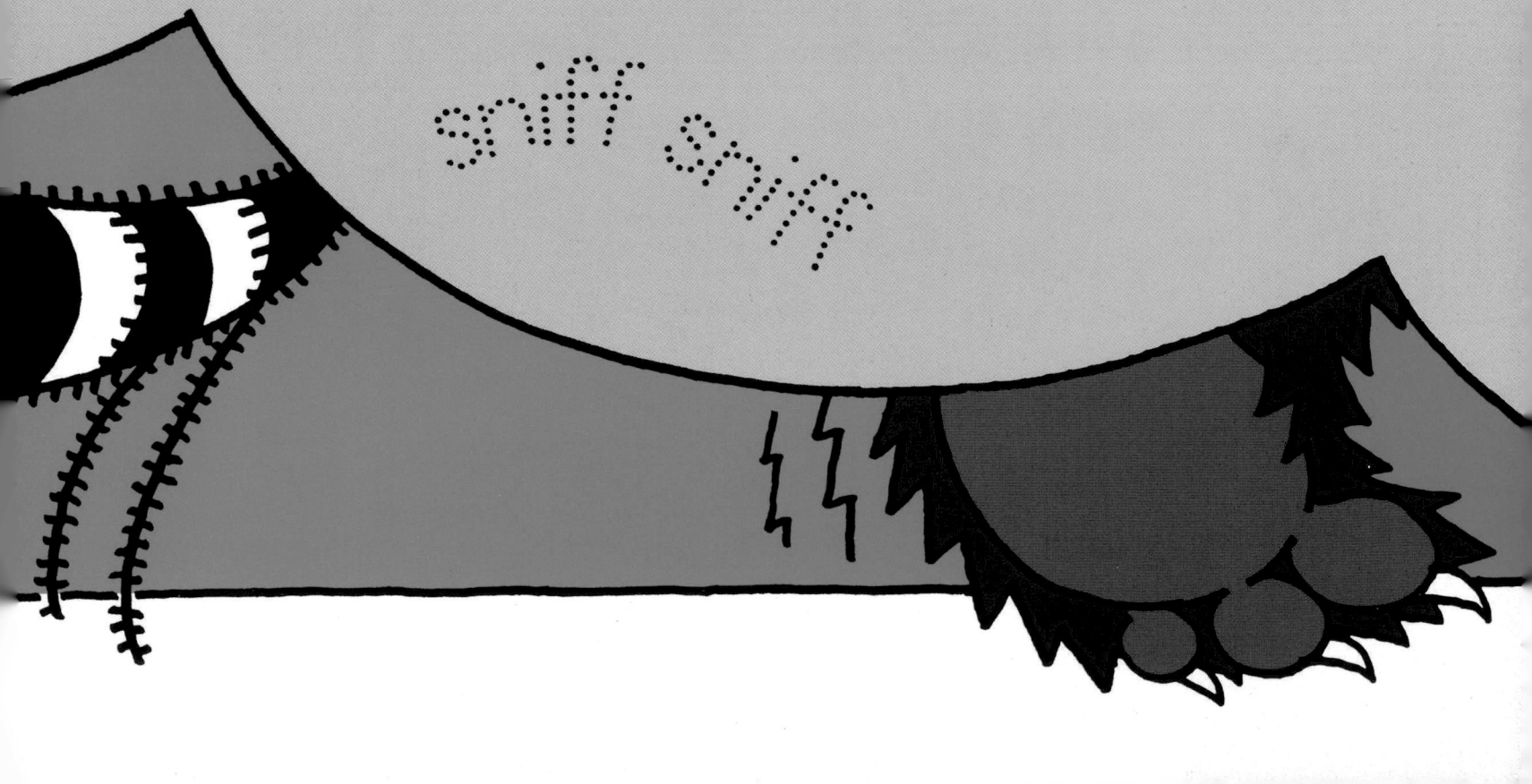

They were lost in the fog

Mog!
Mog!
Is that you?
Sorry
YAK!
BUMP

Iceaxe, compass
Goggles and log
Help me, show me
Lead me to Mog
Oh! here you are
Meg made a spell

The fog started to lift

EEEK!!!
All the fog rolled away

Yeti!
Yak?
Meeow!

They all ran

and
did
not
stop
until
the
top

Mind how you go
Yak

Thanks!
Cheers!
They flew home

It was tea time

WL

Goodbye!